Big Giant
Little Giant

by Liza Charlesworth

ISBN: 978-1-338-78288-2
Illustrated by John Lund
Copyright © 2021 by Liza Charlesworth. All rights reserved.
Published by Scholastic Inc., 557 Broadway, New York, NY 10012

10 9 8 7 6 5 4 3 2 1   68   21 22 23 24 25 26 27/0

Printed in Jiaxing, China. First printing, June 2021.

Big giant can climb a hill.
Little giant can **do** it, too!

Big giant can chop a tree.
Little giant can **do** it, too!

3

Big giant can build a house.
Little giant can **do** it, too!

Big giant can ride a bike.
Little giant can **do** it, too!

5

Big giant can fly a kite.
Little giant can **do** it, too!

Big giant can pick a flower.
Little giant can **do** it, too!

Big giant can make a friend.
Little giant can **do** it, too!